JEMIMA PUDDLE-DUCK'S HILLTOP FARM

MR MCGREGOR'S GARDEN

Jeremy Fisher is a clever and talented frog.

MR TOD & TOMMY BROCK'S WOOD

MY BURROW

DR & MRS BOBTAIL'S BURROW

TUNNEL NETWORK

My friend, Lily Bobtail. Whatever the problem, she's got the answer.

MR BOUNCER'S BURROW (BENJAMIN'S HOME)

RAVINE

DEEP DARK WOODS

DANDELION FIELD

Benjamin Bunny is my cousin. Wherever I go, he's right behind me – usually hiding!

One sunny summer's day in the woods,
Old Brown was in hot pursuit of Squirrel Nutkin.

"STOP, thief!" squawked the owl, flying
straight at the scurrying squirrel.

PETER SAVES THE DAY!

PUFFIN

Map of my woods

This is a map of the woods where I live. You can see who else lives here too. It's in my dad's journal which I always have with me.

ROCKY ISLAND

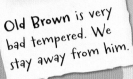

Old Brown is very bad tempered. We stay away from him.

OLD BROWN'S ISLAND

MR JEREMY FISHER'S POND

SQUIRREL NUTKIN'S WOOD

MRS TIGGY-WINKLE'S LAUNDRY

Squirrel Nutkin is always getting into some kind of mischief.

Mrs Tiggy-winkle runs the laundry. She keeps us neat and tidy.

Nutkin tore through the trees, frantically searching for a place to hide. JUST IN TIME, he spotted the door to Peter Rabbit's burrow.

"OPEN UP!" he panted.

Peter opened the door and
Nutkin leapt inside.

"Save me!" he squealed.
"I took Old Brown's glasses . . .
and lost them!"

"Where is that nutty nuisance?"

bellowed Old Brown from outside.

"Don't worry, Nutkin," said Lily.
"We'll help you find them!"

"Phew! He's gone," said Peter, peering out of
the burrow a few minutes later. "Let's hop to it!"

The friends darted through the woods searching for Old Brown's glasses.

"Where do you think you left them, Nutkin?" asked Lily.

"Well . . ." Nutkin thought hard.
"First, I was with Jeremy Fisher."

"Can you see them?" asked Peter as the
friends arrived at Jeremy Fisher's pond.

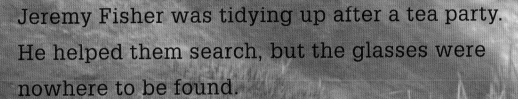

Jeremy Fisher was tidying up after a tea party.
He helped them search, but the glasses were
nowhere to be found.

"Hmm," thought Nutkin out loud, "I did
also go to Mrs Tiggy-winkle's laundry."

Suddenly, a shadow loomed overhead . . .

"Old Brown!" gasped Lily.

"Take cover!" yelled Peter.

As everyone dived under the table, the owl landed on the tabletop – **CRASH!**

"Look! A tunnel!" whispered Lily, pointing. "But can we reach it? Old Brown will catch us."

"We'll take the table with us," said Peter.

The friends used all their strength to lift up the table AND Old Brown.

They crept towards the tunnel.

"Tail feathers!
They're escaping!"
squawked Old Brown.

Nutkin and the rabbits reached the tunnel entrance
and dived inside, as Jeremy sprang away to hide.

"You said you went to Mrs Tiggy-winkle's laundry, Nutkin," panted Peter.

"We'd better go there to look for the glasses. And FAST!"

"Hello, Mrs Tiggy-winkle," called Lily
when they arrived at the laundry.
"Did Nutkin leave some glasses here?"

"Rit-tat-tee, look at me!"
sang cheeky Nutkin, dancing
on a pile of laundry.

"That pesky squirrel didn't leave any glasses," replied Mrs Tiggy-winkle crossly. "Just lots of nasty purple paw prints. Look at my washing!"

Suddenly, they heard a fearful flapping
as Old Brown landed close to Benjamin.

"Got you!" he squawked.

"I should never have led you all into danger," said
Nutkin, bravely jumping in front of the terrified bunny.

"This is bad.
This is really bad!"

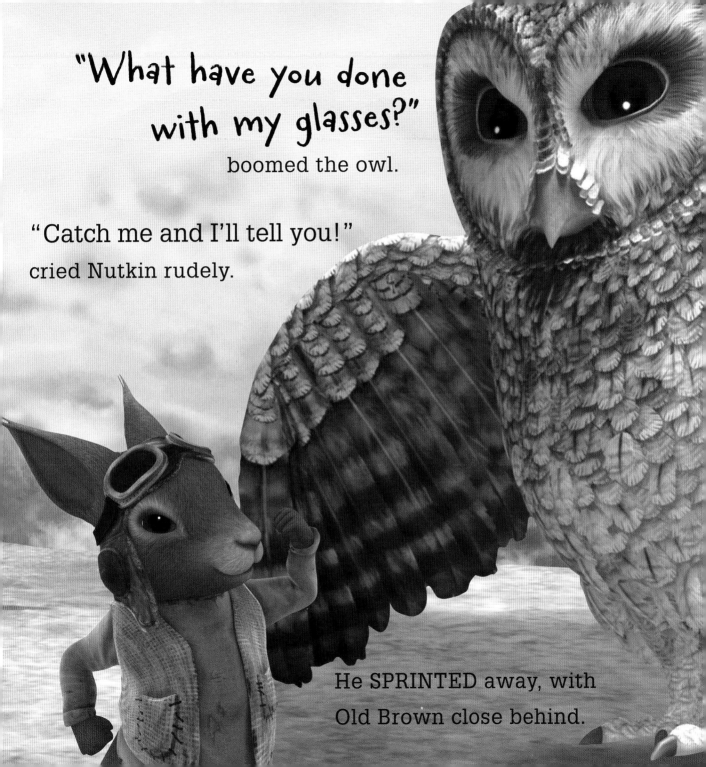

"What have you done with my glasses?" boomed the owl.

"Catch me and I'll tell you!" cried Nutkin rudely.

He SPRINTED away, with Old Brown close behind.

"We MUST find the glasses before Old Brown catches Nutkin!" said Peter. "But how?"

"Nutkin left these purple prints," began Lily. "So . . . what had he stepped in before coming here?"

"BERRIES!" they all gasped together.

The three friends raced off to the blackberry bushes.

"There they are!" cheered
Benjamin, spotting the glasses.

"Great! Now we need to find
Nutkin," said Peter, taking the specs.
"And I know where to look . . ."

As Peter arrived at Squirrel Camp,
he heard a terrible commotion.

Old Brown was
looming over Nutkin...

Peter had to save him!

"WAIT!" shouted Peter, leaping out in front of Nutkin. "I've got your glasses! Nutkin's really sorry he took them."

"Sorry's not good enough," replied Old Brown.

"Then fetch!" shouted Peter, throwing the glasses off the platform.

"Noooo!"

squawked Old Brown, diving
after his precious glasses.

He swooped past Lily
and Benjamin, who were
coming up in the lift, before
catching the specs and flying
grumpily back to his tree.

"Phew, that was close!" said Nutkin. "Thanks for saving me, Peter."

"That's what friends are for," smiled Peter.

"You will try to stay out of trouble now, won't you, Nutkin?" said Lily.

Do **YOU** think he will?

OLD BROWN'S TREE

I've never seen inside but the squirrels are always sneaking around there. Old Brown gets SO angry if he catches them! Here's a squirrel sketch from my dad's journal.

Landing branch

← To Squirrel Camp –
I mile as the owl flies

Squirrel tail
(maybe it's
Nutkin's?)
Pull twig to ring bell
(and annoy Old Brown)
MORE books
- boring!
Precious glasses
Dusty old book
Good hiding spot
DANGER -
creaky twig!

Making TRACKS!

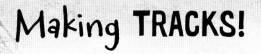

Lily worked out where to find Old Brown's glasses by following Nutkin's trail of berry footprints.

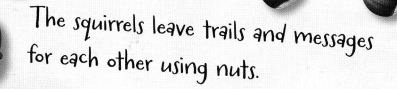

The squirrels leave trails and messages for each other using nuts.

Make a trail for a friend to follow using pebbles or scraps of paper. Use these symbols to leave messages:

Let's hop to it!

Want to go on an adventure?

Catch me if you can!

CONGRATULATIONS!

SKILL IN TRAIL-FINDING CERTIFICATE

Awarded to

_____

_____

Age

_____

Peter Rabbit

PETER RABBIT
BEST TRAIL-FINDER IN THE WOODS

Tip-top
trail-finding
skills!